ISBN 979-8-9853105-8-0

This book is dedicated to
the most tremendous tutors of
them of all,

Nanny Peggy,
Granny Maggie, and
Aunty Rita

River and the Tremendous Yellow Wellie Tutors

written by
Emily Dreeling

illustrated by
Misha Jovanovic

Another chilly fall evening, and Bertie, Lexie, Miley, and Teddy, are feeling the cold wafting in under the front door.

"Crikey! You'd think they'd
stick the heating on, wouldn't you?
It's FREEZING down here!" says Lexie, shivering.

"You can write that one down," answers Bertie.
"I'm about to turn BLUE!"

"We all will if this weather keeps up!
It's not even winter yet, and do you hear that wind
whistling outside? It'd wake the dead!" says Teddy.

"Ehh...I'm not so sure that's the wind," says Miley,
craning toward the half-open living room door.
"It's River...SHE'S CRYING!"

Lexie gasps. "Dear me, you're right!
We'd better see what's happening."

Hopping inside, the four find
her doubled up on the couch, sobbing.

"River, River, what's the matter? What's WRONG?!" says Bertie.

"Nothing, nothing's wrong. I'll be okay in a moment.
I'm f-f-f-fine, hon-honestly," she says, struggling
to hold back the tears.

"Fine, MY EYE!" Lexie replies. "Listen, we've known you
since you were knee-high to a grasshopper and we can tell
when something's up. So - WHAT'S GOING ON?"

Alarmed by her silence, Bertie presses the issue.
"Oh PLEASE tell us River, we're beside ourselves here!"

1 + 1
3.14159265358

"I'm sorry. I don't want to worry you," she answers, wiping her nose on her sleeve. "But...it's just SO embarrassing."

"What is?" asks Lexie.

"I'm getting picked on...because...well, because...I'm HORRIBLE at math! And, and, it's just AWFUL...because I'm so bad with numbers... and adding, and subtracting. I just can't do it. I just CAN'T! I'm HOPELESS! And NOW...now, it's even worse because of how badly I'm being teased about it."

"Oh River! I know it must seem terrible, but please try not to get too upset," says Miley. "Remember everyone learns at different paces. I mean, think about how incredible you are with your reading. And writing too! I bet most in your class aren't half as good as you are yet - so don't panic about the math stuff, it'll come to you eventually."

"Well, it can't come soon enough!"
she says, still sniffling.

"You'll see - it won't be long till you get the
hang of it," says Teddy reassuringly. "So for the
time being, pay no attention to those bullies - they're
just jealous of how smart you are."

"Hmm...I guess you're right -
I'll try to ignore them," River replies.
"Thanks for the advice, I feel a bit better now.
Okay, I gotta get some study done,
I have a test tomorrow."

"Say no more," says Miley,
"we'll leave you to it. Good luck!"

The next day she bursts into the hallway howling, and it's clear to everyone that - unlike them - it's not the temperature that's bothering her.

"LOOK! AN 'F', A BIG, FAT, 'F' FOR 'FAILED'! I TOLD YOU, I'M JUST USELESS - A TOTAL LOSER!" she says, waving her test paper furiously back and forth in front of them. "And now the taunting is TEN TIMES as bad - today was THE WORST!"

"Oh, I'm so sorry River - HOW DREADFUL! But I'm sure it'll all come out in the wash," says Lexie, attempting to console her.

Having the opposite effect, she becomes even more hysterical, prompting Murphy - who's been busy trying to keep the draft off the little wellies - to ask River who it is that's giving her grief.

"It's that nasty girl next door.
She's the one who started it all, and now
there's a whole gang who won't leave me alone
because of her. Why does it matter anyway?!"
she says. "Bullies! They're ALL the same!"

"Uhh... ahh... yup, fair enough,"
says Murphy, taken aback. "I was just curious."

"UGH, curious! How about saving these questions
for another day? Now's REALLY not a good time!"

Murphy opens his mouth to apologize, but doesn't
even get the chance to speak.

"HUMPH! Just forget it - I'm going to my room!"
she says, hollering over the sound of her footfall
thunderously hitting the steps in twos and threes.

"WHOA!" he says, hearing
her door slam upstairs.

"'WHOA', is right!" says Teddy.
"I think it's come off its hinges!"

"Er...it looks like she might have too," says Bertie,
picking his jaw up off the floor. "THIS IS BAD!"

"UH-HUH!" says Miley. "And seeing as yesterday's
advice was clearly rubbish, we need another solution -
or better yet, A MIRACLE - to fix this. Umm...now
what can we do? Let's think everyone - and FAST!"

A frenzy of head scratching begins.

After an in-depth study of the cracks
in the ceiling, Lexie is the first to make a suggestion.

"I KNOW! Why don't we teach her ourselves?"

"I LIKE IT!" says Teddy. "But how will we
do it so she'll understand everything easily and
not wind up even MORE frustrated?"

In her element, Miley pipes up.

"I really like it too, Lexie! And Teddy, it's simple, all we've
got to do is make it FUN! For instance, we could pretend to
be the numbers, and she can add us, subtract us – whatever!
We'll take it slowly to begin with, and hopefully the
game will be such a hoot that it'll inspire her to
give the harder sums another go."

1+1=
2+2=
5-2=

Bertie is the first to grasp what she means.

"Ah, so, one wellie plus one wellie equals two wellies?"

"EXACTLY!" says Miley. "And five wellies minus three wellies leaves us with two wellies...that sort of thing."

Fully cottoning on, all three whelp with joy.

"But, we're going to need some help," Miley continues, as she turns to address Pearl, Polly, and Priscilla, whom she's caught listening.

"Hey, you lot up there! Can you be our math symbols? We need to make the plus, minus, and equal signs on the floor, and you'd be perfect!"

Annoyed their earwigging has
gotten them accidentally roped in, the three
nosy parker's pretend not to hear her at first.

Miley, however, has them sussed. Placing
her hands on her hips, she makes it clear with
her poutiest pout she won't be going quietly -
and that an answer is due.

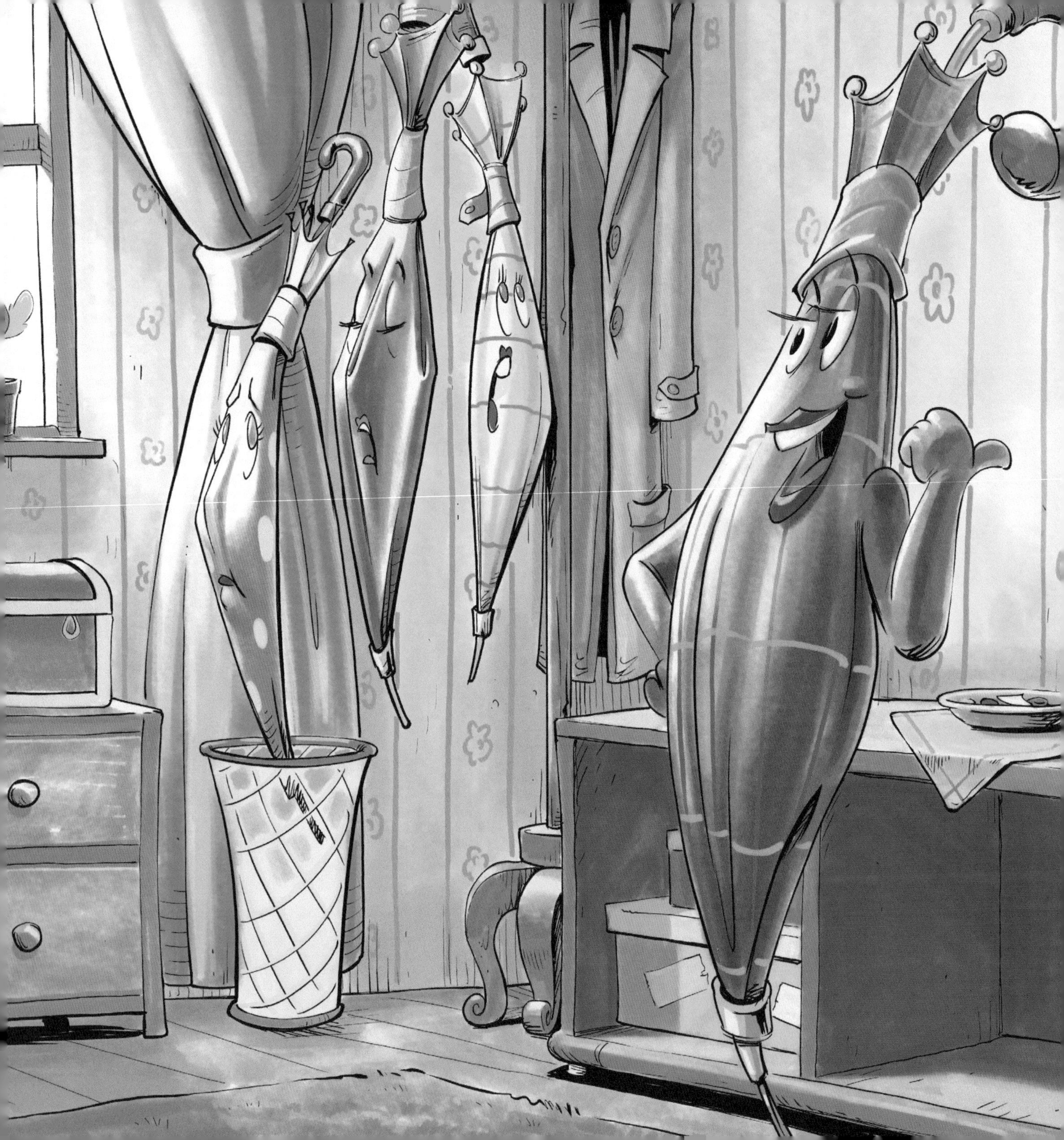

Following a long, awkward
pause, Pearl is the first to decline.

"Yeah...thanks for the offer, but I think I'll take a
rain check on this one – I've zero interest in math."

"Same here," says Polly. "I've always thought numbers
were kind of pointless – so it's no can do, I'm afraid."

"You can count me out too," says Priscilla, putting the boot in.
"I can't add or subtract to save my life. And despite how hard
I tried to get the knack of it, the penny never seemed to drop."

Taking everything in from her prized spot by the front door,
Trudy can't wait to throw her two cents in.

"Why, it's just as well you're all no great shakes in that
department – because judging by the look on Murphy's
face I wouldn't fancy being able to tot up the amount
of days I'd left on that hanger if I were you!"

Murphy - whose gaze is now fully trained in their direction - starts snarling at them, and in an instant, they completely change their tune.

"Oh, alright, alright!" says Pearl. "But if you ask me, it's all a HUGE waste of time. It'll be just like Priscilla's case - if she can't do it now, she never will."

"HUH! Luckily, no one did ask you," Trudy replies. "And just because Priscilla had trouble, it doesn't mean River will. Everybody's different.

"Anyway, you should be thrilled to help – it's not like you three are up to much these days. You're so old and tattered no one even brings you out anymore. Next stop's the bin, so you may as well make some good use of the time you've got left.

"You know what, Miley?" she goes on. "You won't be able to make all the symbols you need without a fourth umbrella, so I'd only be too glad to step up and do my bit."

"Jeepers, you're right,"
she says, after thinking it over. "We'll definitely take you up on that, thanks! It's going to be an all hands on deck effort for sure - so Murphy, could you bring all the brollies to the treehouse at lesson time, then act as lookout for River's folks while we're teaching?"

"EH...WHY THE TREEHOUSE? NO ONE SAID ANYTHING ABOUT THE TREEHOUSE WHEN WE AGREED TO ALL THIS!" says Pearl, quivering at the thought of being carted around by their number one enemy.

"Because there's too much risk of being caught here in the hallway," Miley explains. "There are big people coming and going all day long, and it'd be impossible to get anything done with all the stopping and starting we'd have to do - we wouldn't be able to concentrate!

"Okay Murphy, is it a 'yes'?"

"No need to ask twice," he answers,
then smacks his lips at the trembling trio.

"And ladies, we're good to go?"

"OH SURE! We can't wait to be in the clutches
of the hound from hell down there!" says Polly.

"We must be mad!" says Priscilla.

"MAD? MAD? IT'S DOWNRIGHT CRAZY!" says Pearl.
"And I'm telling you right now, young Miley - and
actually all of you do-gooding lot too - should anything
happen to us, never let it be known that we went willingly...
or... or... OR... WE'LL COME BACK TO HAUNT YOU!"

"For goodness sake, CALM DOWN!"
Miley tells them. "Murphy's been through intensive
anti-brat therapy with Teddy for ages, and he's a completely
reformed character these days. Right, Murphy?"

"Born-again!" he replies devilishly. "There's nothing to fear
lassies, I'll take REAL good care of you."

Teddy rolls his eyes, while the rest of the little wellies giggle
at the three of them now clinging to each other
for dear life.

"SERIOUSLY? HAUNT US?!" says Trudy, joining in on the
laughter. "You do realize you torment us, morning, noon,
and night, anyhow? Truth be told, I think we'd have
a lovely bit of peace and quiet here if
Murphy took off with you witches
once and for all!"

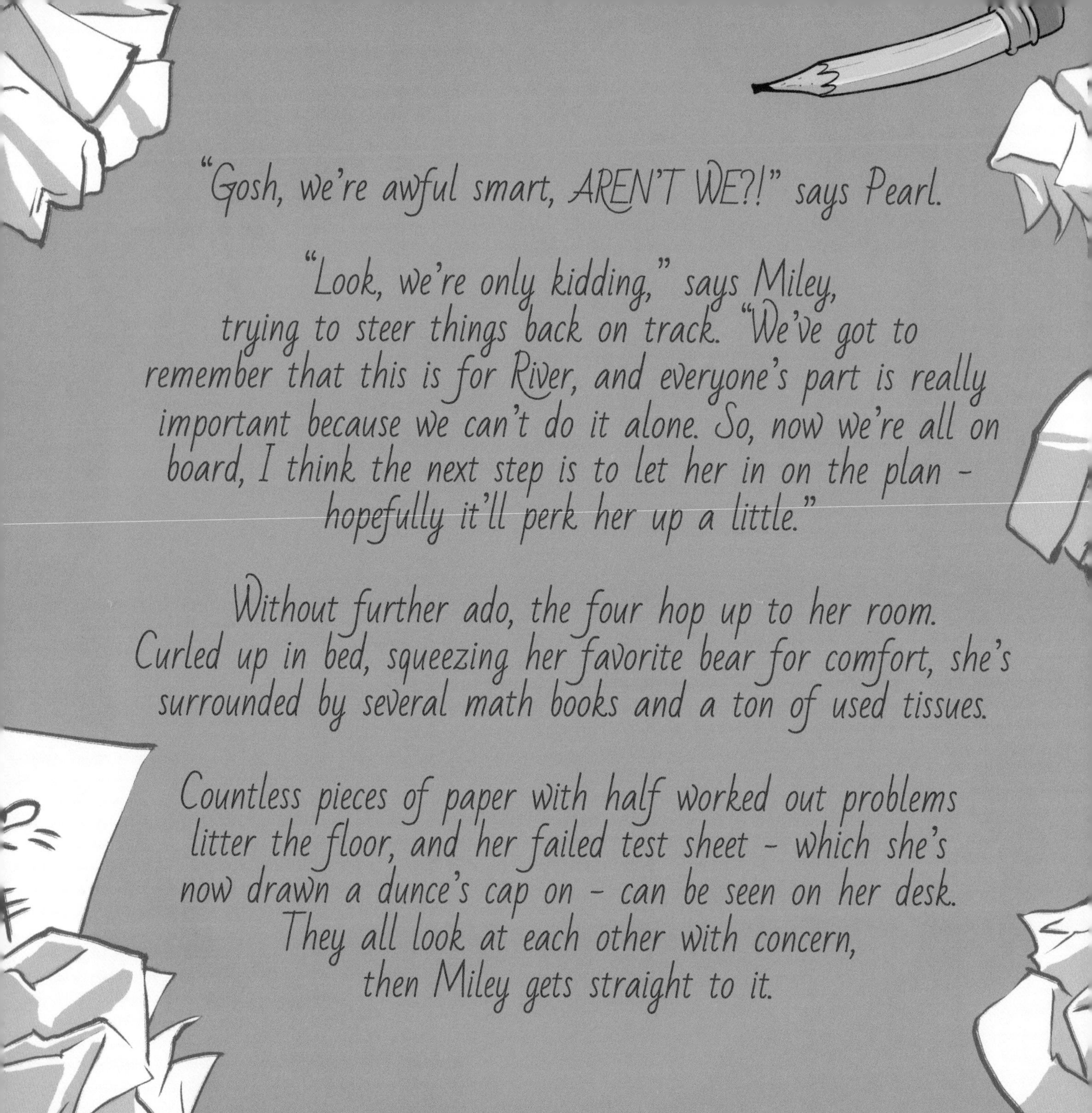

"Gosh, we're awful smart, AREN'T WE?!" says Pearl.

"Look, we're only kidding," says Miley, trying to steer things back on track. "We've got to remember that this is for River, and everyone's part is really important because we can't do it alone. So, now we're all on board, I think the next step is to let her in on the plan - hopefully it'll perk her up a little."

Without further ado, the four hop up to her room. Curled up in bed, squeezing her favorite bear for comfort, she's surrounded by several math books and a ton of used tissues.

Countless pieces of paper with half worked out problems litter the floor, and her failed test sheet - which she's now drawn a dunce's cap on - can be seen on her desk. They all look at each other with concern, then Miley gets straight to it.

"Hey River! Guess who's here?!
Only your favorite booties - and we've an amazing idea to help you with your math!"

"Well whatever it is, forget it," she replies. "I've already tried my best and I still can't make head nor tail of it all - I'll never be up to scratch."

"But that's not true," says Miley. "You're so far ahead with your reading and writing already - and once we show you this new way of doing numbers, you'll be clued-up on that front in no time."

"Stop making such a fuss about my reading and writing - anybody can do that! I'm telling you, no matter what magic cure you think you have, this can't be fixed.

"I'm just going to have to live with all the nastiness, and be miserable, fuh...fuh...forever..." she says, while motioning them to leave. "Can you close the door behind you? I need some time alone."

2+2=5
5-3=3
3+2=

DO NOT DISTURB!

Gobsmacked, the group
turn on their heels and walk out.
Hearing her cry again, their hearts break.

"Oh jeez, oh jeez," says Bertie, starting to fret.
"How are we going to sort THIS?!"

"Heaven knows," says Lexie, sighing. "Those
rotten bullies have really gotten under her skin."

"It's unbelievable," says Teddy. "She sounds exactly
like those three old hags in the hallway -
as if she's totally given up!"

"HOLEY SOLES! It's a MUCH bigger problem than we all thought," says Bertie, vibrating. "We need to go back to the drawing board and find another solution as quickly as we can. OH GOSH – I'm SO worried about her!"

"Me too!" says Lexie.

"Me three!" says Teddy.

"And me!" says Miley. "That rascal next door has a LOT to answer for. Erm...okay – how about this time round we just focus on lifting her spirits? She's completely down in the dumps, and unless we can brighten her mood, she'll never give our math lessons a go."

12%
10% +

"Neat thinking Miley, but how on EARTH
will we manage THAT?!" says Bertie,
now in the throes of a full-on tizzy.
"It'll be next to IMPOSSIBLE!"

In an effort to calm him, Lexie steps in.

"I know it's terribly upsetting Bertie.
Given how glum she is, it's going to be quite a task -
but it sounds like Miley has something up her sleeve
that might change River's mindset..."

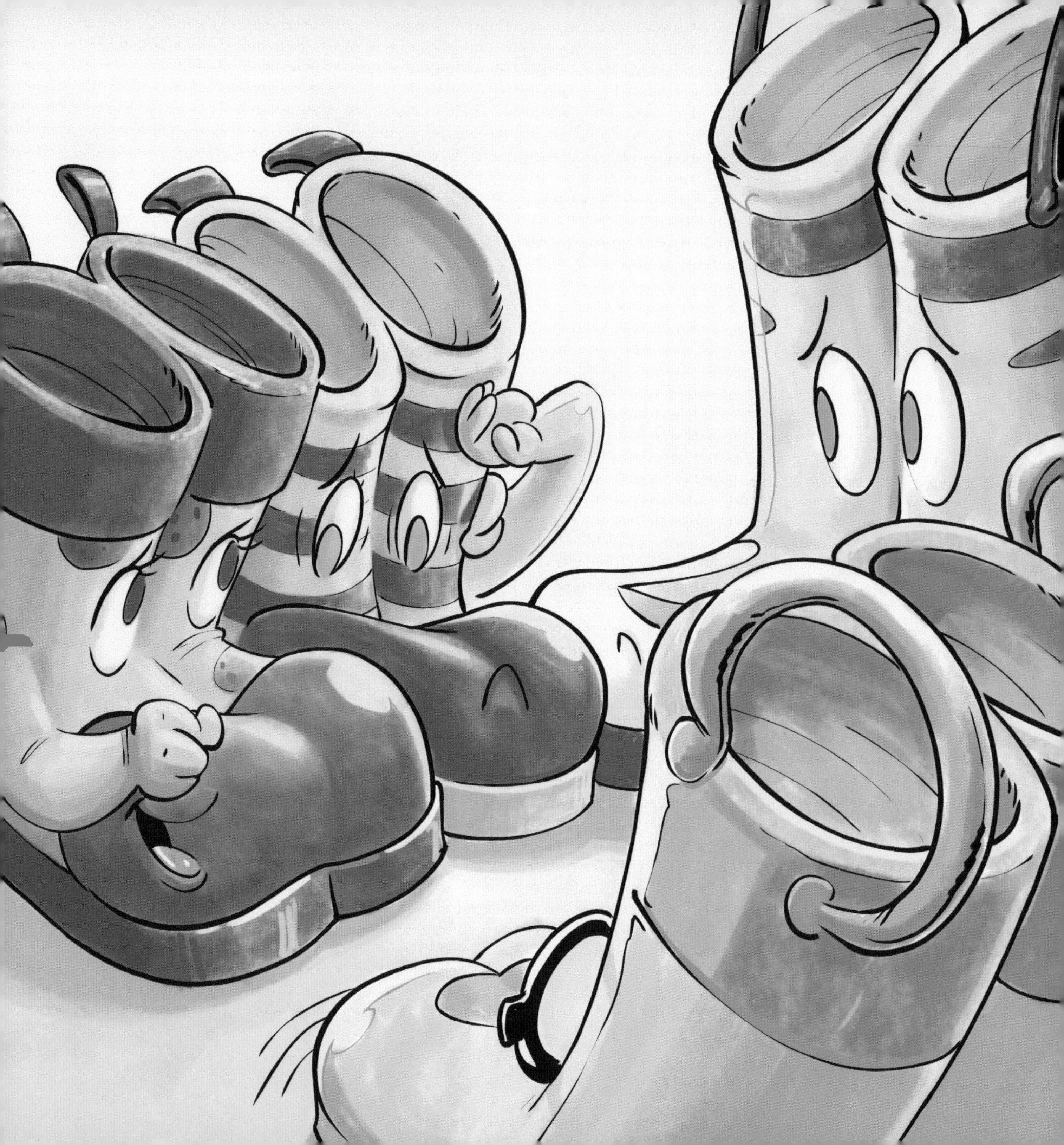

"As it happens, I DO!" Miley replies chirpily. "She's been so bogged down with all this extra study that she hasn't been out in the garden with ages - and I think it'd do her the world of good to be in nature for a while. Being amongst the plants, animals, and birds, is sure to put her back in good form."

"GENIUS!" says Lexie. "And who better than us four to show her a good time outside?!"

"No kidding! It's exactly what we were made for – especially on days like these," says Teddy. "We'll have so much fun together, she'll hopefully see that in the big scheme of things this bully doesn't matter a jot."

"PRECISELY!" says Miley. "Righto, here's the drill. We'll play with her one at a time, and while doing so, we'll slip some useful tips into each conversation to help her get through all of this. Then – fingers crossed – by the time we're finished she'll feel more capable, confident, carefree, and cheerful, than ever!"

Lexie punches the air. "Miley, IT'S A WINNER! Because when all's said and done, some of the best lessons are the ones that can't be learned from books."

"You said it, Lexie! And I already have a way to show her how capable she really is," says Teddy excitedly.

"Fantastic! I'll take charge of the confidence boost then – that's right up my street!" she replies.

"Okay, that leaves you and me, Bertie," says Miley. "And, no offence, but I think I should work on the carefree side of things with her."

"None taken," Bertie answers. "I mean, I'm very happy buzzing around the place when I'm not freaking out, about like, EVERYTHING! Yeah, I reckon the cheerful part is definitely best left to me."

They all laugh, but it's not long
before Bertie gets flustered again.

"OH JEEZ! We forgot something MAJOR!" he says, throwing his hands in the air. "Exactly HOW are we going to lure her outside?! All this is pretty useless if we can't get her to budge!"

"URGH! I hate to admit it, but you're right," Lexie says. "She hasn't set foot in the yard since Teddy's disappearance a few weeks back. I remember she started school a couple of days later, and it all went downhill from there. We'll obviously have to think of something else - Miley, where's the flip chart you had earlier?"

"Not so fast!" says Teddy, cutting in. "It might stun you all to know that every so often I have a lightbulb moment. And fortunately for us, I had one just as I was thinking about proving to River how capable she is."

"BY GUM – you really are FULL of surprises!" Lexie says teasingly. "Go on then, give us the scoop!"

"Yes, do tell, Teddy – I'm DYING to know what you've come up with," says Bertie, barely able to contain himself. "Hurry Miley – bring that chart thingy over here so he can fill us in at once!"

"Yeah, yeah, on the way," Miley replies, sounding slightly miffed that her thunder has been stolen.

Handing over her markers, Teddy starts scribbling on a fresh page, while the trio anxiously await the lowdown.

"Lexie, you mentioned earlier that River
hasn't gone out since the day I went missing, right?
And you said she was super worried about me, right?
And that she couldn't rest until I was back home safely, right?"

"Er...right-t-t...," they answer, clearly
wondering what direction he's taking them.

"Right! Well, I'm going to plant myself firmly in that
bed of muck below her bedroom window. And you lot are
going to run upstairs and be all hysterical and stuff,
and tell her I'm sinking, and that there's no way
I'm getting out of it alive without her help.

"Meanwhile, I'll be screeching like crazy, and she'll
be so spooked, she'll come running right into my arms -
and BOOM! - right into lesson number one!"

Lexie grins. "YUP, that'll do the trick!"

"Agreed! Although, I'm not sure I like the thought of giving her such a fright," says Bertie, clutching his chest. "My nerves couldn't take it!"

"I'm not a fan of that part either, Bertie. But this is a crisis situation, and we gotta do what we gotta do," replies Miley matter-of-factly. "And Teddy, you truly are full of surprises. Remind me to pick your brain the next time disaster strikes."

"It'd be an honor!" says Teddy, beaming. "Okey-doke! Now we're all clear on our next move, we should skidaddle - we've got a TON of work to do!"

"For real!" says Lexie. "You two - LET'S GO! Okay, we'll see you in a bit Teddy, and BEST OF LUCK!"

Waving goodbye, Teddy heads for
the back door, while Bertie, Lexie, and Miley,
get revved up for their big entrance. Soon after,
they charge upstairs like a herd of elephants and
barge straight into River's room. Jumping up and
down like mad, while pointing frantically at her
window, the three start yelling and screaming.

"Look, look...LOOK! River, you have to come!
It's Teddy, he's in real deep trouble this time,
and we can't rescue him without you!" says Lexie.

"YES! We need you, River - NOW - or we'll
NEVER get him out!" says Miley.

"And then he'll be STUCK," says Bertie,
"FOR ALL OF ETERNITY-Y-Y..."

Instantly leaping from the bed
to the sill, River is horrified by the sight
that greets her. Teddy is wailing and moaning,
with his hands in the air one minute, then down
in the mud the next, trying to push himself out.

Seeing him struggle, River gasps, and without
hesitating she pulls Lexie on one boot at
a time, snatches her coat, and runs.

High-fiving each other, Bertie and Miley
immediately race after them.

Outside, Teddy is still
putting on quite a performance.

"HELP, HELPPPPP, SOMEBODY HELP! PLEASE!
I'M SINKING! HELP! IS ANYBODY THERE-E-E?!"

"It's okay, Teddy - I'M HERE! We'll have you
out in a jiffy," says River, rushing to his side.

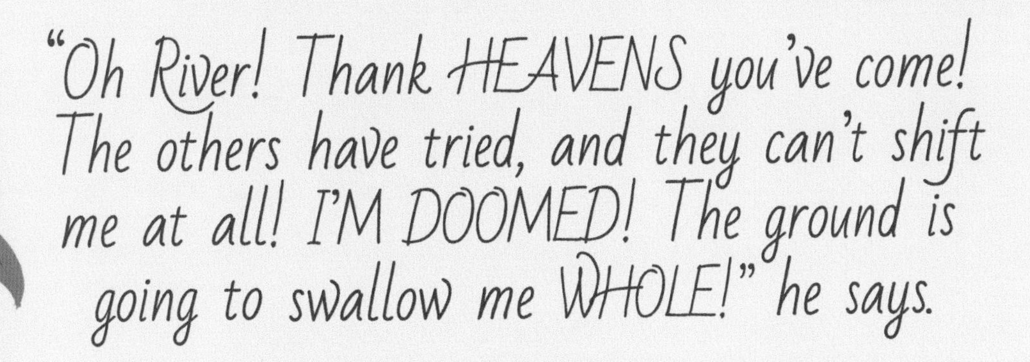

"Oh River! Thank HEAVENS you've come!
The others have tried, and they can't shift
me at all! I'M DOOMED! The ground is
going to swallow me WHOLE!" he says.

"Not if I have anything to do with it.
Just hold on, my friend -
WE'VE GOT THIS!"

Grabbing him by his bootstraps,
River plants herself firmly in the earth
and starts tugging with all her might. Secretly
winking at Lexie, Teddy deliberately digs himself
in a little deeper with each pull. On and on it goes,
but she doesn't give up. Rocking forward and back,
Teddy at last stops resisting, and on her next
yank he pops clean out of the wet clay.

Suddenly uprooted, River flies backwards into the air.
And to everyone's amazement, she manages to land
with Teddy still firmly in her grip.

"TEDDY - WE'VE DONE IT! WE'VE SAVED YOU!"
she says, hugging him giddily.

"'WE', haven't done anything," says Teddy.
"This was all YOU, and you alone."

Glancing around, River sees Bertie and Miley on the sidelines, and realizes he's right – that she's done it all by herself.

"I can't believe it," she says, gulping. "I thought I'd told you two to grab Teddy's arms and pull with me, but I must have forgotten to say something in the frenzy of it all."

"Nope, you didn't say a word. You simply rolled up your sleeves and went straight to work!" says Bertie.

"We'd have stepped in had you needed us," Miley adds, "but you didn't, because you're a superstar!"

"A superstar – and MY HERO!" says Teddy fondly. "I'll be forever in your debt for freeing me, and I only hope this makes you see how capable you are. I knew I was safe the minute I saw you, because you can do anything you set your mind to, you know – you really can!"

"Oh Teddy, you've no idea how much that means to me," she replies. "But I don't know about being able to do just anything. Like – how am I ever going to get you and Lexie all cleaned up?! It's going to take the rest of the day, and I still have so much homework to get through!"

"HAH - don't worry about that, kid!
Just march me on over to that puddle by the treehouse,
and we'll have it taken care of in a flash," says Lexie.

"Great, because I can't be out here much longer,"
River says. "And besides, I'm feeling kinda
chilly now I've stopped moving."

"I hear you," Lexie tells her,
"but I promise we'll be done in two shakes."

Moments later - with Bertie, Miley, and Teddy,
in tow - they reach the pool. It's brilliantly clear from
the last downpour right before they rushed into the garden.

Catching a glimpse
of herself in it, River's heart sinks
upon noticing she's all covered in dirt too.

"EWW...look at me, I'm in such a state. No wonder
I haven't got any friends. If I can't even take care of you
guys without making a complete mess of it - and myself
into the bargain - then I'm not surprised I'm being
pushed around and called names. They're right,
I'm just a NINCOMPOOP!"

As tears begin to well in her eyes, Lexie decides
to get lesson number two directly underway.

"River, you mustn't listen to that nonsense -
it's entirely untrue! Look, I know you're
in a hurry, so let's jump in now and
we'll talk later."

Not giving her a second to change
her mind, Teddy – on Lexie's cue – grabs hold of
River's hand and charges her straight into the water.

"C'mon Bertie! C'mon Miley!" says Lexie.
"IT'S TIME TO PARTY!"

Like lightning, the pair dive in – then all
four start bouncing up and down like yo-yo's.

"C'mon River, stomp those feet! STOMP, STOMP, STOMP!
C'mon, we're almost spotless!" she goes on.

Thoroughly enjoying all the splishing and splashing,
River traipses over every inch of the puddle
until she finally wears herself out.

"Oh Lexie, I'm BEAT – I need to
sit down for a bit."

"Of course!" Lexie replies.
"Let's put our feet up by the edge here
and gather ourselves."

Drained from all the excitement, the rest of the
crew follow them out and plop down beside each other.

"MY, OH, MY - you're nearly as good as NEW!" says River,
seeing Lexie and Teddy are now perfectly spick and span.

"Told you it wouldn't take long - and I bet you never
thought you'd have so much fun scrubbing us down?!"
says Lexie, chuckling.

"I certainly DIDN'T! It was such a buzz -
but, how come it was SO easy?"

"Well," Lexie answers,
"one of the best things about
being waterproof is that none of
the bad stuff soaks in. It sticks to the
surface for a while alright – but it NEVER
seeps through – because once we remember what
we're made of, it slides off in a snap!"

"Ahh," says River. "Not in a million years would
I have thought of that – but now you mention it,
it makes perfect sense."

Staring into the pool, she sees her image once again.
Now everyone's out, the water is still, and clearer than
ever, and River realizes the mud has completely run
off her also after all the frolicking about.

BAD STUFF

"Seems I've washed up real nice myself,"
she says, admiring her fresh, rosy-cheeked face.

"YOU SURE DID!" says Lexie heartily. "But just for the record, whether you're cloaked in muck or not - there's no such thing as a bad reflection where you're concerned."

River starts to glow. "Oh stop it Lexie, you're embarrassing me!"

"My dear, I'm only stating a fact. Now - all you have to do is remember this view before you, and you'll be forever confident as to how truly lovely you are, both outside and in!"

"I'll try - promise I will," says River, gazing deeply into the puddle. A short spell passes, then she gets up to leave.

"Okay...I gotta get going, but that was a BLAST!
Thanks everyone!"

Keen to get lesson number three in motion before she disappears, Miley jumps in front of her.

"Wait, WAIT!" she says. "If you think that was a scream, let me show you something even better."

"Eh...I don't think so. This day is just slipping by, and I've got nothing done," River replies, now sounding a little antsy.

"Honestly, I don't want to hold you up, but this will be over before you know it - cross my heart!"

"Oh alright! I suppose another few minutes out here won't hurt me."

"THAT'S THE SPIRIT!" says Miley. "Can you take Lexie off then, and put me on instead?"

"Sure thing," says River. "So...where are we off to?"

"I thought you'd never ask!
See that huge leaf pile over there by the shed?
On the count of three, we're going to plow right into it."

"BRILLIANT!" River says, lighting up at the notion.

"Ready?! Here we go! ONE, TWO..."

Bubbling with excitement, River doesn't even wait for Miley to finish before she takes off like a shot. Once she nears the heap, she skids like a daredevil straight into the bottom of it. Leaves scatter everywhere, and they both roll on the ground in stitches.

"WHAT A RIOT!" she says, shouting at the top of her lungs. Then, spotting the mess they've made once she stands up, River goes into a spin.

"Miley! The lawn is a SHAMBLES!
Ronnie will show his teeth when he sees what we've done. QUICK – let's grab that wheelbarrow beside the swing before he comes out!"

"Listen, don't worry about Ronnie. If he does surface, maybe we'll convince him to give it a try as well. Some hijinks would certainly do him a world of good – he's the most uptight rake I've ever met!"

"Yup," says River, "always on edge. Which makes me even more nervous about what he'll say – he must have spent hours gathering all this up!"

"That's true," Miley says. "Tell you what, why don't we have another quick run around and kick up all the little bundles we seem to have made? Then we'll get everything back in order before Ronnie appears – the mound will be just as he left it. Pinky swear!"

"Mmm...okay – I guess it's no harm while they're all over the place."

"My sentiments exactly! Hey, speaking of stuff being upside down - you know, my favorite thing to do is close my eyes and think of all the things that have been bothering me lately. And I imagine each leaf in a clump being one of those worries - either big, small, or in-between."

"Really? Then what?" asks River.

"Then, I charge full speed ahead and give them a good boot in the air - and somehow, magically, all my troubles seem to vanish. You should try it out - seriously, it WORKS WONDERS!"

"You're joking me?! Agh...FINE - I'll have a go," she says, shutting her eyelids warily.

As she's lost in thought, Miley notices her face getting redder and redder. Reaching peak traffic light a few seconds in, she roars.

"I'M SOOOOO READY - LET'S RIP!"

2-2
y
z
7 +
=
4
3

Again, Miley barely has a chance to collect herself before she bolts. And in the blink of an eye, stack after stack goes flying high into the air until there's nothing left to strike. Flopping down on the grass afterwards, River lets out a huge sigh of relief.

"WOWEE – I'm soooo calm. With all the hassle I've been having at school lately, it's like a dream. Way to go, Miley, this was THE BEST!"

"No worries! I'm so happy you were able to unwind a little," she replies. "Always keep in mind though, River, that you're only ever a hop, skip, and jump away from being completely carefree at any time."

"GOOD! Because right now I see a whole bunch of grief coming our way," she says, pointing shakily towards the shed.

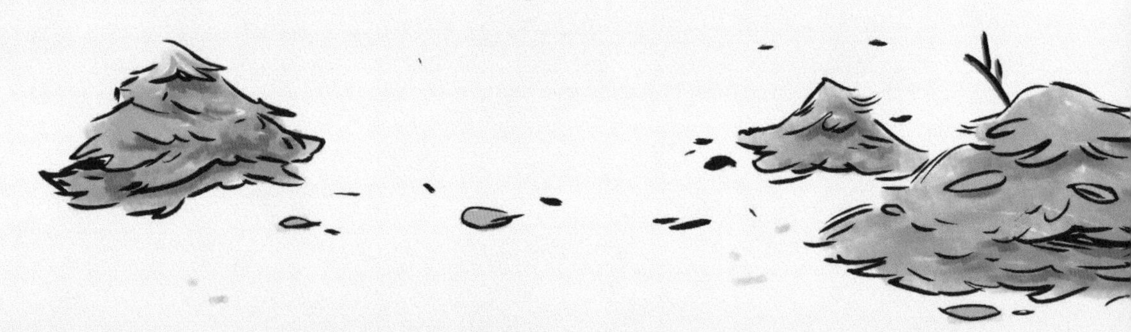

Peering over, Miley sees Ronnie has popped
outside the door to where Bertie, Lexie, and Teddy,
have been patiently waiting for the lesson to end.
He's blinking like crazy at all three of them.

"BLIMEY! It's worse than I thought. He's going absolutely berserk over there," says River. "WHAT ARE WE GOING TO DO?!"

"Listen – what we're NOT going to do is have a meltdown," says Miley, attempting to lower the temperature. "NOPE! The wisest thing is to find out what's actually happening first before we go jumping to conclusions."

"SHEESH! Let's just hope we live to tell the tale then, eh?" she says, still clearly on the brink.

"Oi, Lexie! Everything okay?" Miley mouths over to her.

"Er...yeah," she mouths back, looking puzzled. "Why?"

Miley throws a side-eye towards Ronnie.

"Oh, no, he's fine. Walter's just driving him bananas looking for tea and biscuits every five minutes, so he's delighted you've given him an excuse for a break with all the raking that needs to be done."

"PHEW!" says River, at last breathing easily.

"Now, what was I saying?" asks Miley. "Things are never as bad as they seem. And even if they do get a little hairy on occasion, panicking is utterly pointless. It's better to go kick up your heels instead, safe in the knowledge everything will work out in the end."

"You're so right, Miley. I'll try not to let anything get on top of me from now on. And if it does, I'll know exactly where to come."

"THAT'S MY GIRL!" Miley says.

Just then, a storm cloud
moves overhead and some droplets begin to fall.

"YUCK - RAIN!" says River. "I'm going inside before it lashes - thanks again for such a fun afternoon, folks."

Starting back towards the house, she suddenly hears Bertie hollering for all he's worth.

"STOP! STOP IT! HOLD ON THERE!
HOLD ON!"

The fuss halts River in her tracks, and Bertie finally catches up to her.

"Bertie, WHAT NOW?! I really must be off!"

Sensing he's now truly on borrowed time, Bertie begins stuttering under the pressure.

"Eh...ah...a-a-any chance you could stand still for a second? And...er...ah...look straight up at the s-sky?"

"JEEPERS - I'm calling it a day, Bertie! For real, I'm trying to avoid another drenching here, if you don't mind!"

"But...but...River, y-y-you'll be back inside in a tick - you have my w-word."

River purses her lips, and Bertie
goes into begging mode knowing lesson number
four is - without question - on the line.

"PLEASE, PLEASE, PLEASEEEEEE! PRETTY PLEASE,"
he says, waving his clasped hands wildly in the air.

Eventually giving in, she tuts, then tilts her head back.
Drizzle quickly dampens her face.

"Doesn't it feel AMAZING?" asks Bertie.

"It feels...it feels - simply wonderful, and...so strangely
refreshing," she replies, trying to catch some drops
on her tongue.

Minutes swiftly slip by while she soaks up the
experience - enjoying it to such an extent she
doesn't realize the showers have stopped.

"YIPPEE! Blue skies again!" Bertie says.

River snaps out of her daydream. "HEAVENS - it's SO bright!"

Rays of white light warm her face, and she smiles widely.

"Bright, and BEE-AUTIFUL!" he replies with a hum. "You know what the best thing about rain is?"

River shakes her head.

"No matter what, sunshine ALWAYS follows. Bad weather comes and goes, just like bad times do. So, even when our world seems like it's been turned on its head, we've got one good reason to stay cheerful - and it's that happiness is right around the corner!"

"Hmm...when you put it like that Bertie, I certainly feel a lot more content knowing this sad spell won't last forever."

"River, that's MUSIC TO MY EARS!
I think my work here is done, but before I buzz off and leave you in peace, know that we'll always be here for you – through thick or thin. And that we'll always keep you safe."

"It stinks we can't go to school with you every day, but try and find someone who has a bunch of little yellow wellies they love to hang out with at home as well, and you'll have surely found another great friend!"

"Ohh...B-B-Bertie!" she says, blubbing. "I'll always be here for you too, and for Miley, and Lexie, and Teddy – to pull you out of a jam, to play, or just press pause for a moment when you need some time out."

Calling the rest of the crew over, River gathers them all in for a cuddle.

"NOW CAN WE GO IN?!" she asks jokingly.

Everybody laughs, then they head back to the hallway hand in hand. Inside, Miley decides to take advantage of her good mood.

"Hey River, just thought I'd mention those math lessons are still up for grabs..."

"Is that so? Well...if that's the case - then I'll definitely take you up on them!"

Delighted their plan has worked, the four do a stealth victory dance once she turns to hang up her coat.

"YAY - I CAN'T WAIT! We're gonna be the most tremendous tutors you've ever had," says Miley, unable to stop shimmying with all the excitement. "Let's start tomorrow after school."

"IT'S A DATE!" replies River.

Time goes by. And through their nightly trek to the treehouse with Murphy and the four umbrellas, they soon have River up to speed with her sums. Adding and subtracting each other over and over again, they make sure with enough practice that she's all set for her next test.

"I GOT AN 'A'!" she says, as she climbs up the last rung of the ladder to share her result.

They all cheer ecstatically.

"We KNEW you could do it!" says Miley, grinning from ear to ear.

"Not without your help, I couldn't. Thanks guys, I owe you one!"

"No need to thank us, River - that's what friends are for. But tell us, what's it like being TOP OF THE CLASS?!" says Lexie.

"I mean...it's nice and all. Now that I'm better than them at solving problems, the bullies have totally backed off. But even if things were still the same, I wouldn't care a fig what they had to say now anyway."

A

"Interesting! Why's that?" Bertie asks.

"Because...I know it's amazing to be really good at something, but what does it matter if you don't love doing it too, right? And this whole thing has made me realize that you shouldn't let other people make you feel bad about yourself, or the things you enjoy the most.

"From now on, I'm going to find others who adore reading and writing just as much as I do - and stop wasting my time worrying about kids that I've zero in common with anyway!"

"HEAR! HEAR!" says Teddy. "We're SO proud of you!"

"Oh give over, you lot, you're making me blush! ANYHOO, I have to run, I've got this new book that I can't wait to get stuck into - it's this crazy story about a little boy who's best buds with all his sneakers."

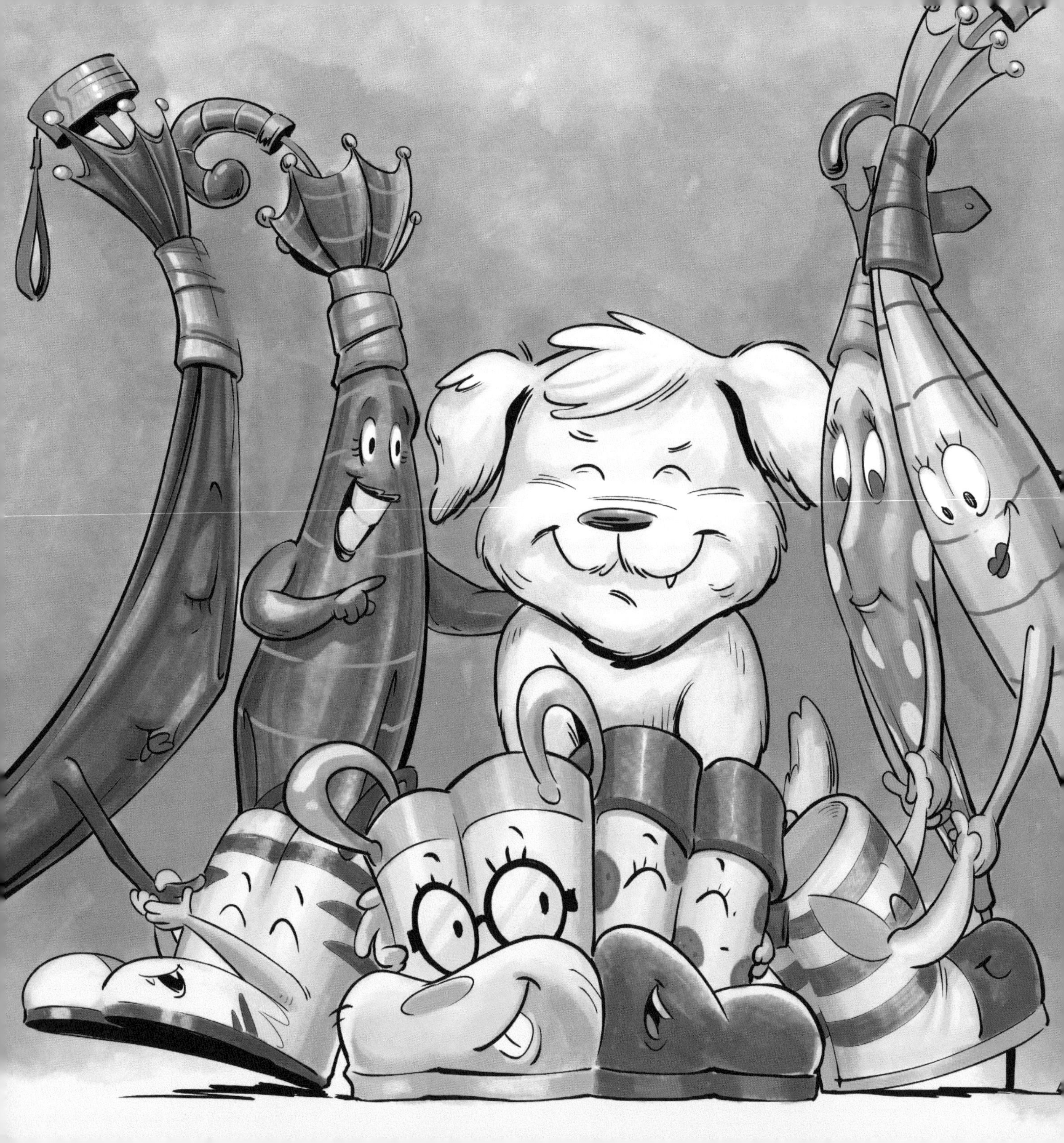

After she's gone, the little treehouse tutors
all pat each other on the back, thrilled they've been able
to help her, and that she's back to her usual self once more.

"AHEM! So y'all know, River's not the only one
walking on air around here," Murphy says smugly.

Lexie makes a face. "What do you mean?"

"Well, I think it's fair to say that - as promised - I've been
taking great care of the brollies these past few weeks..."

"Credit where credit's due," says Pearl, butting in. "We had
a few hairy moments alright, but for the most part
he's managed to keep his paws to himself."

"But," Murphy continues,
"I'd be lying if I said it wasn't a struggle.
And you three most likely would've been toast only for
we all needed to pitch in to make this work..."

"I KNEW IT!" says Polly.

"ROTTEN TO THE CORE!" says Priscilla.

"SHUSH!" says Trudy. "LET HIM FINISH!"

"...HOWEVER, since you ladies were out of bounds, I had to
let off steam somehow. Then I remembered it was the girl
next door who started pestering River in the first place –
so I decided to go on a little excursion. And guess
who has four pairs of little red wellies?"

Teddy groans. "Good grief –
NOW what have you been up to?!"

"Why, I've only been having the best fun EVER, old chum. And I know from all the anti-brat sessions we've had that I've probably crossed the line again, but this time I thought you'd go easy on me given everything River's been through."

"Look, if it's any consolation, we don't give a monkey's what you did..." says Pearl.

"...so long as it wasn't to us!" says Polly.

"AMEN TO THAT!" says Priscilla. "But I reckon I speak for everyone when I say that we can't wait to find out how they got their comeuppance."

"Good, because you're gonna LOVE it!" he answers. "Okay – it all went down a few nights ago when I snuck through the cat flap. There they all were, fast asleep on the shoe rack, ready for the taking. I had to pinch myself to make sure it wasn't a dream.

"But when I realized everything was real, I knew I had to get to work quickly before anyone stirred. Like lightning, I chewed through the soles of the first pair. Then I filled the second up with kitty litter. The third was tied together, and I buried the fourth out in the sandpit.

"Afterwards I wondered had I gone a little over the top, but any doubts I had on that front went straight out the window when I saw the look on that little scallywag's face the next morning – it was ABSOLUTELY PRICELESS! So, I think it's safe to say that all's well that ends well!"

They all roll around the floor in hysterics.

"Oh Murphy - I think
it's also safe to say you're totally off the hook,"
replies Teddy, buckled over. "But let's just hope she doesn't
find out it was us who did it, or we could be in
for some real trouble."

"Yeah, I'm pretty sure none of them will talk - but if they
do, I know we can handle it. Just look at how well we took
care of things this time. I say a big old-fashioned bear hug
is in order for a job brilliantly done!"

And with that, everybody comes together in a solid
embrace, now happier than ever knowing
River is happy again too.

...The End

Printed in Great Britain
by Amazon